BENJAMIN BEAR

IN

FUZZY THINKING

PHILIPPE COUDRAY

ABOUT THE AUTHOR

PHILIPPE COUDRAY loves drawing comics, and his many children's books are often used in the schools of France, his home country. In fact, his work was chosen by students to win the prestigious Angoulême Prix des Écoles. Philippe's twin brother Jean-Luc is also a humorist, and they relish any opportunity to collaborate on children's books and comics. Although he lives in Bordeaux, Philippe does not especially like wine. He does enjoy painting, creating stereoscopic images, and traveling to Canada, where he looks for Bigfoot. Though he continues to search each year, Benjamin Bear will always be his favorite wild animal.

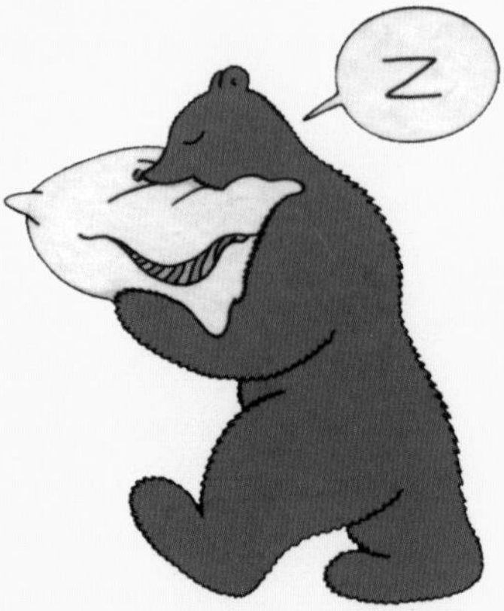
Z

BENJAMIN BEAR

IN
FUZZY THINKING

A TOON BOOK BY
PHILIPPE COUDRAY

Also look for: *Benjamin Bear in Bright Ideas!*
Benjamin Bear in Brain Storms!

The Benjamin Bear books have received the following accolades:

ALA NOTABLE CHILDREN'S BOOKS 2014
BOOKLIST'S TOP 10 GRAPHIC NOVELS FOR YOUTH 2014
A JUNIOR LIBRARY GUILD SELECTION 2013
ALA CHILDREN'S GRAPHIC NOVEL READING LIST 2013
EISNER AWARD BEST PUBLICATION FOR EARLY READERS NOMINEE 2012 & 2014
WINNER OF THE YOUNG READERS PANDA AWARD 2012-2013
NEW YORK PUBLIC LIBRARY'S 100 TITLES FOR READING AND SHARING 2011

For Robert, Debbie, and their children

Editorial Director: FRANÇOISE MOULY

Book Design: FRANÇOISE MOULY & JONATHAN BENNETT

PHILIPPE COUDRAY'S artwork was drawn in India ink and colored digitally.

A TOON Book™ © 2011 TOON Books, an imprint of RAW Junior, LLC, 27 Greene Street, New York, NY 10013. Original French text and art © 2010 Philippe Coudray and La Boîte à Bulles. No part of this book may be used or reproduced in any manner whatsoever without written permission except in the case of brief quotations embodied in critical articles and reviews. TOON Books®, TOON Graphics™, LITTLE LIT® and TOON Into Reading™ are trademarks of RAW Junior, LLC. All rights reserved.

Library of Congress Cataloging-in-Publication Data: Coudray, Philippe.   Benjamin Bear in Fuzzy Thinking : TOON Level 2 / by Philippe Coudray   p. cm.   Summary: Although he is a very serious bear, Benjamin Bear has a funny way of doing things, like drying dishes on a rabbit's back or sharing his sweater without taking it off.   ISBN-13: 978-1-935179-12-2 (hardcover)   1. Graphic novels. [1. Graphic novels. 2. Bears--Fiction. 3. Humorous stories.]   I. Title. II. Title: Fuzzy thinking.   PZ7.7.C68Be 2011 741.5'973--dc22   2011000801

All our books are Smyth Sewn (the highest library-quality binding available) and printed with soy-based inks on acid-free woodfree paper harvested from responsible sources. Printed in China by C&C Offset Printing Co., Ltd. Distributed to the trade by Consortium Book Sales & Distribution, a division of Ingram Content Group; orders (866) 400-5351; ips@ingramcontent.com; www.cbsd.com.

ISBN 978-1-935179-12-2 (hardcover)   ISBN 978-1-935179-25-2 (paperback)

20 21 22 23 24 25 C&C 12 11 10 9 8 7 6 5 4

www.TOON-BOOKS.com

A big fish

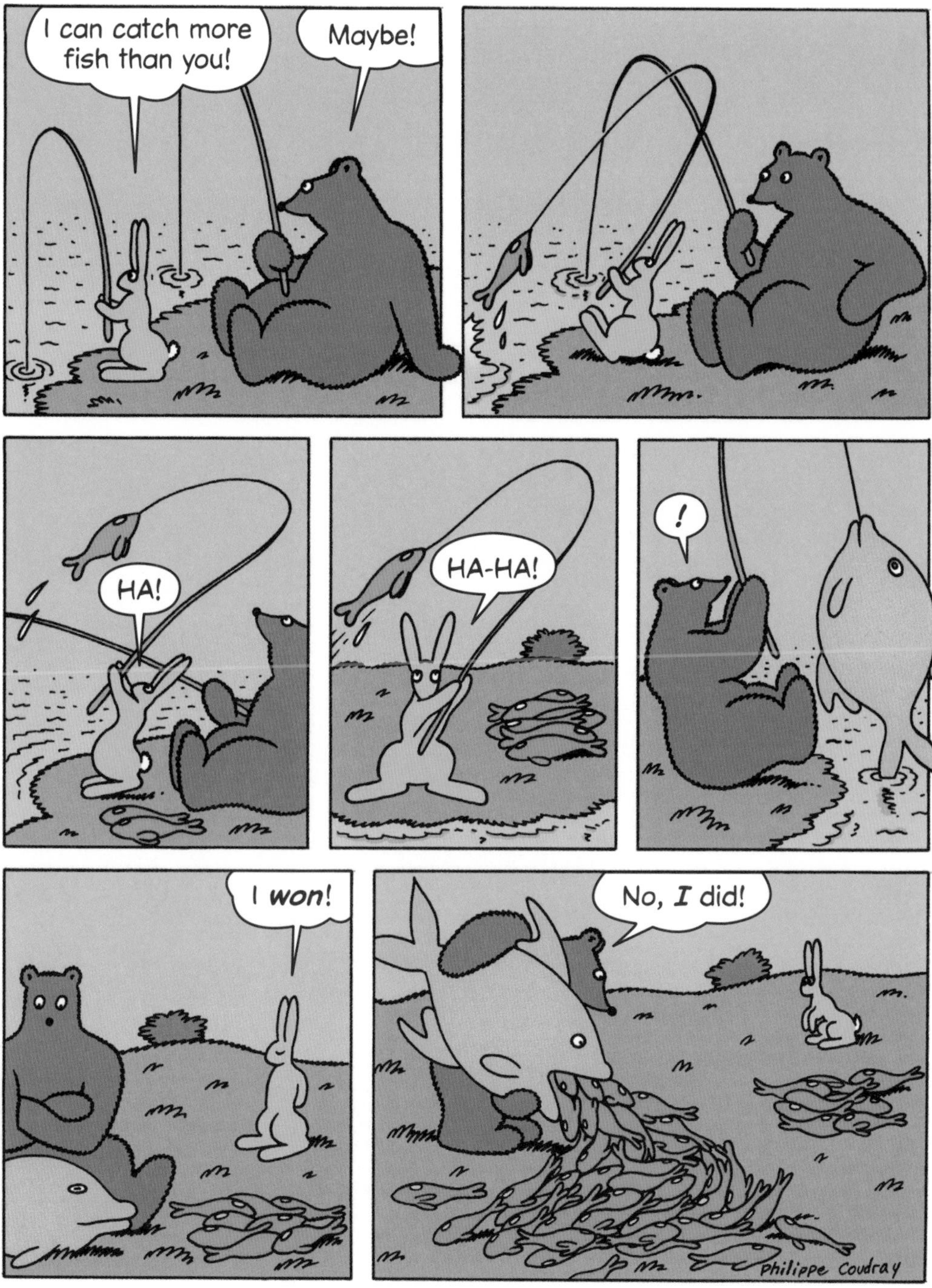
I can catch more fish than you!
Maybe!
HA!
HA-HA!
!
I **won**!
No, ***I*** did!
Philippe Coudray

Cold night

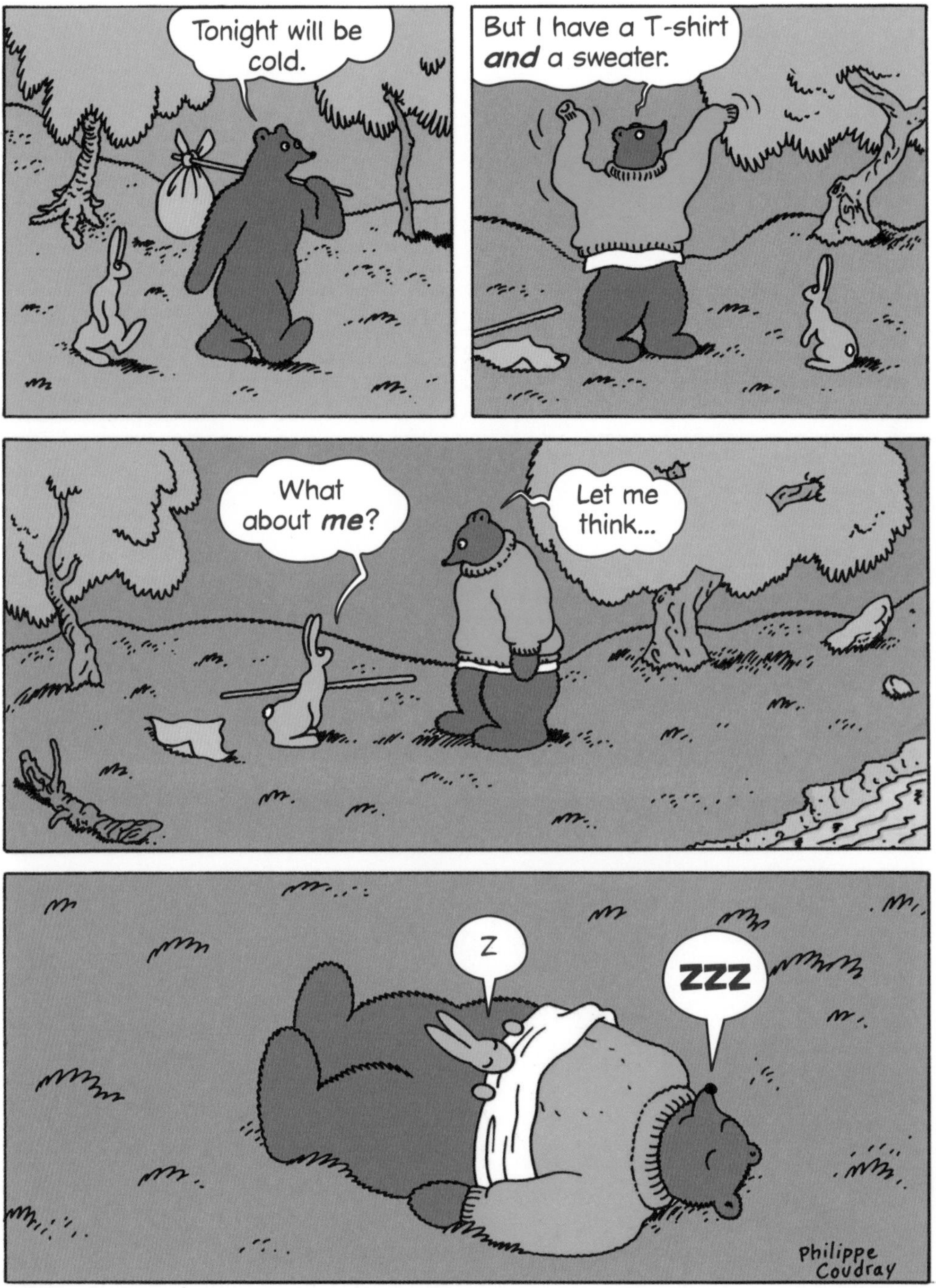

Tonight will be cold.
But I have a T-shirt **and** a sweater.
What about **me**?
Let me think...
Z
ZZZ
Philippe Coudray

Painting

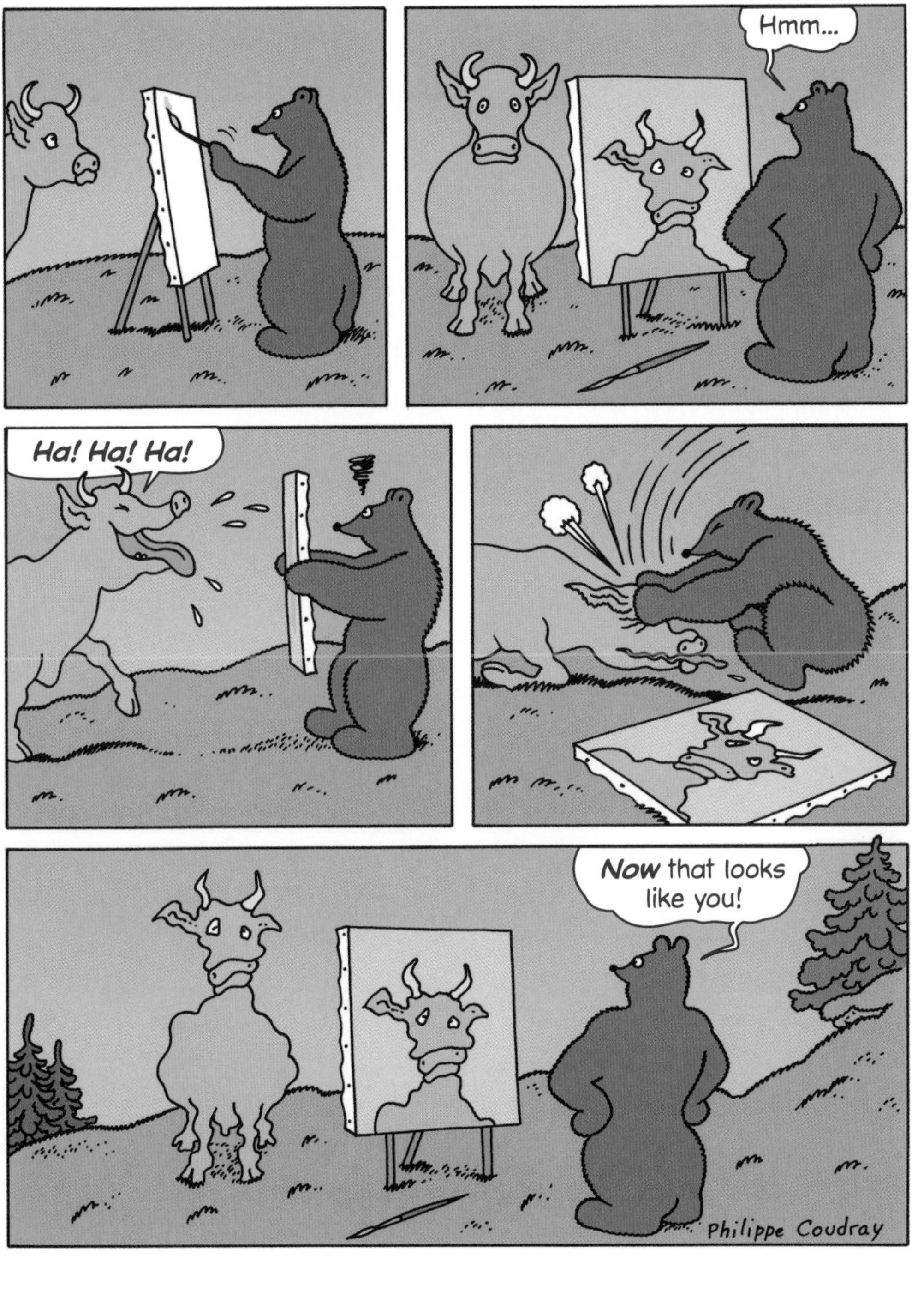
Hmm...
Ha! Ha! Ha!
Now that looks like you!
Philippe Coudray

Tall tree

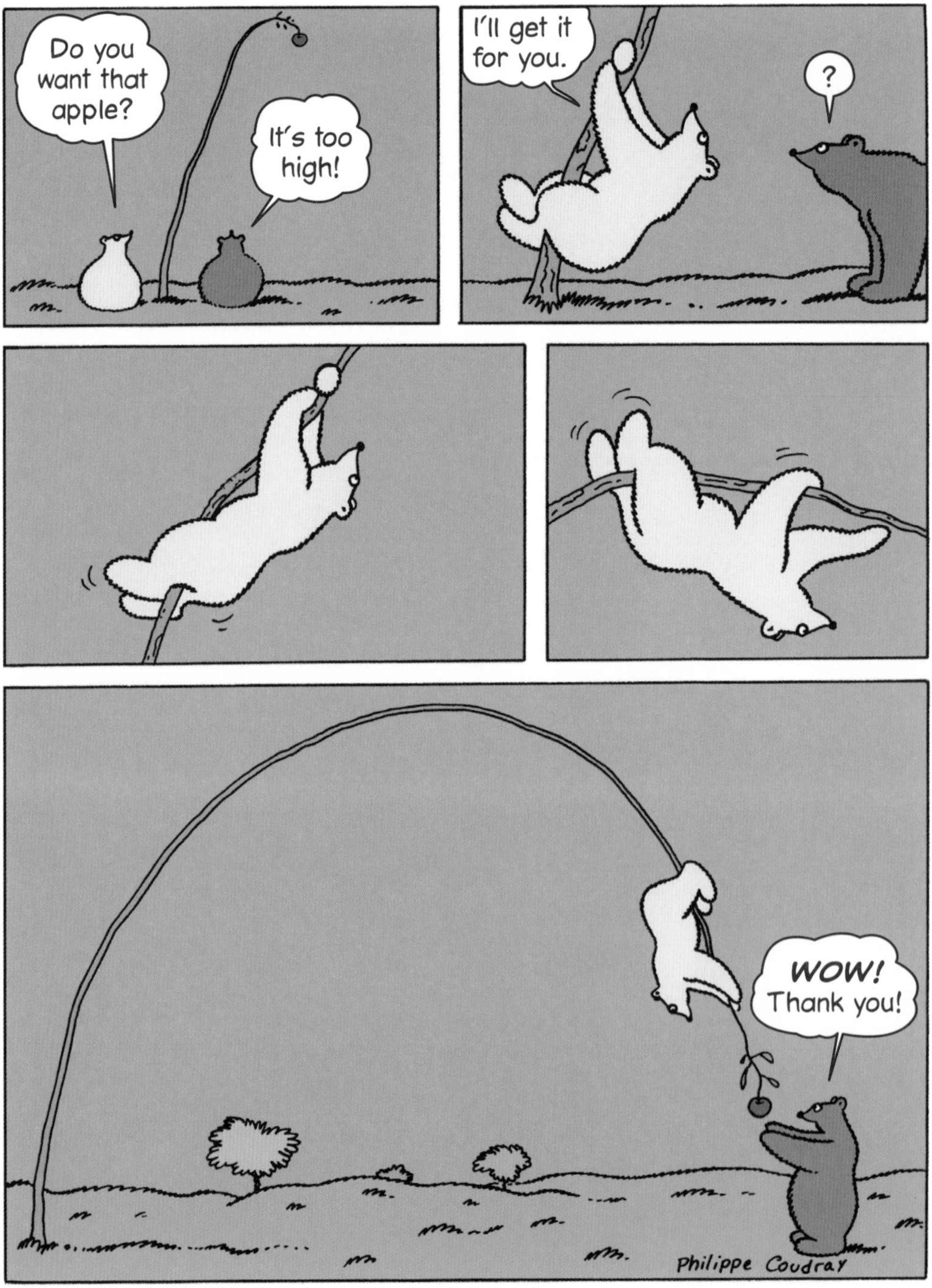
Do you want that apple?
It's too high!
I'll get it for you.
?
WOW! Thank you!
Philippe Coudray

Karate

Philippe Coudray

9

To fly—or not

Philippe Coudray

10

A long nap

Philippe Coudray

The man in the moon

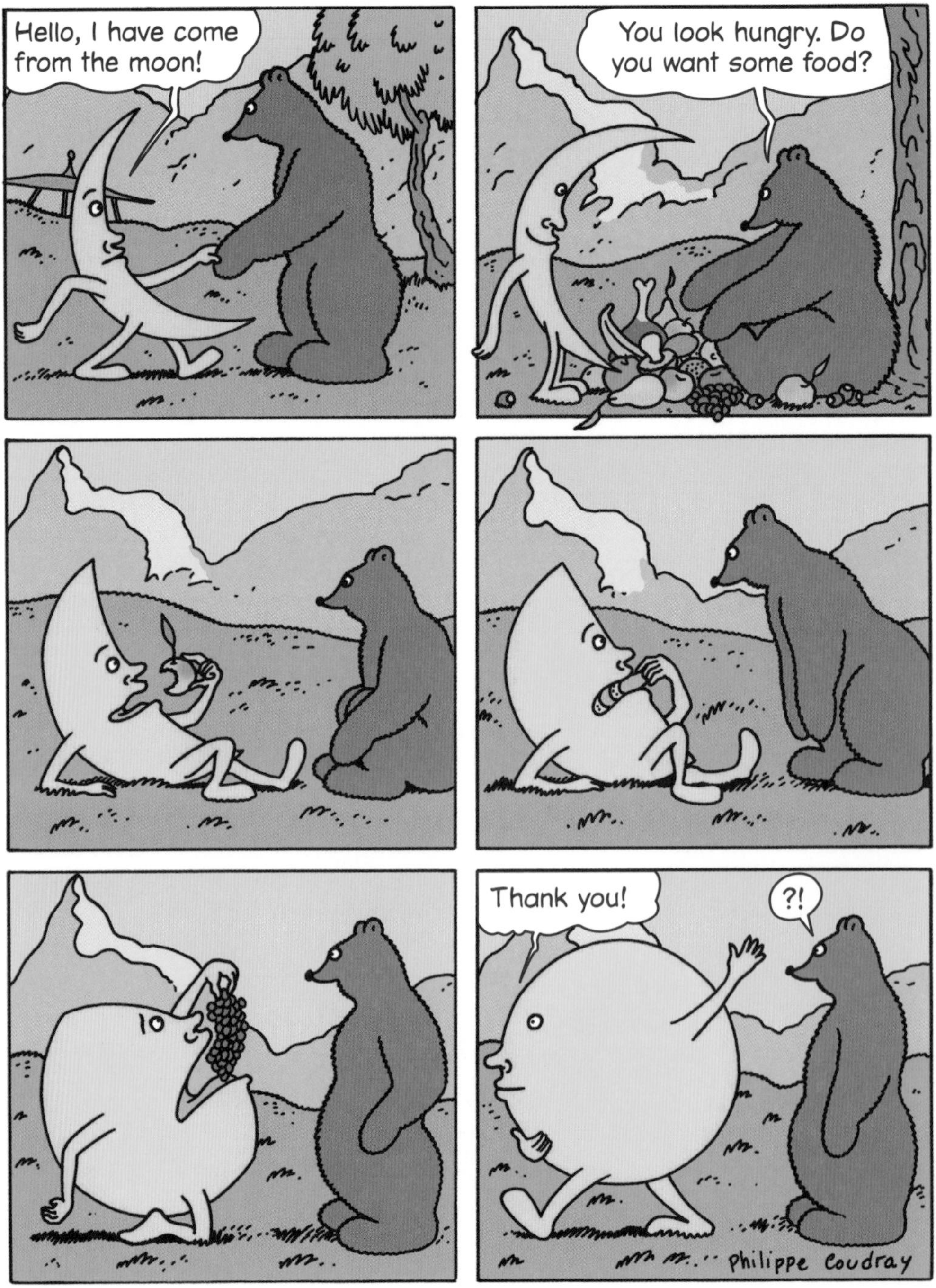
Hello, I have come from the moon!
You look hungry. Do you want some food?
Thank you!
?!
philippe coudray

Underwater

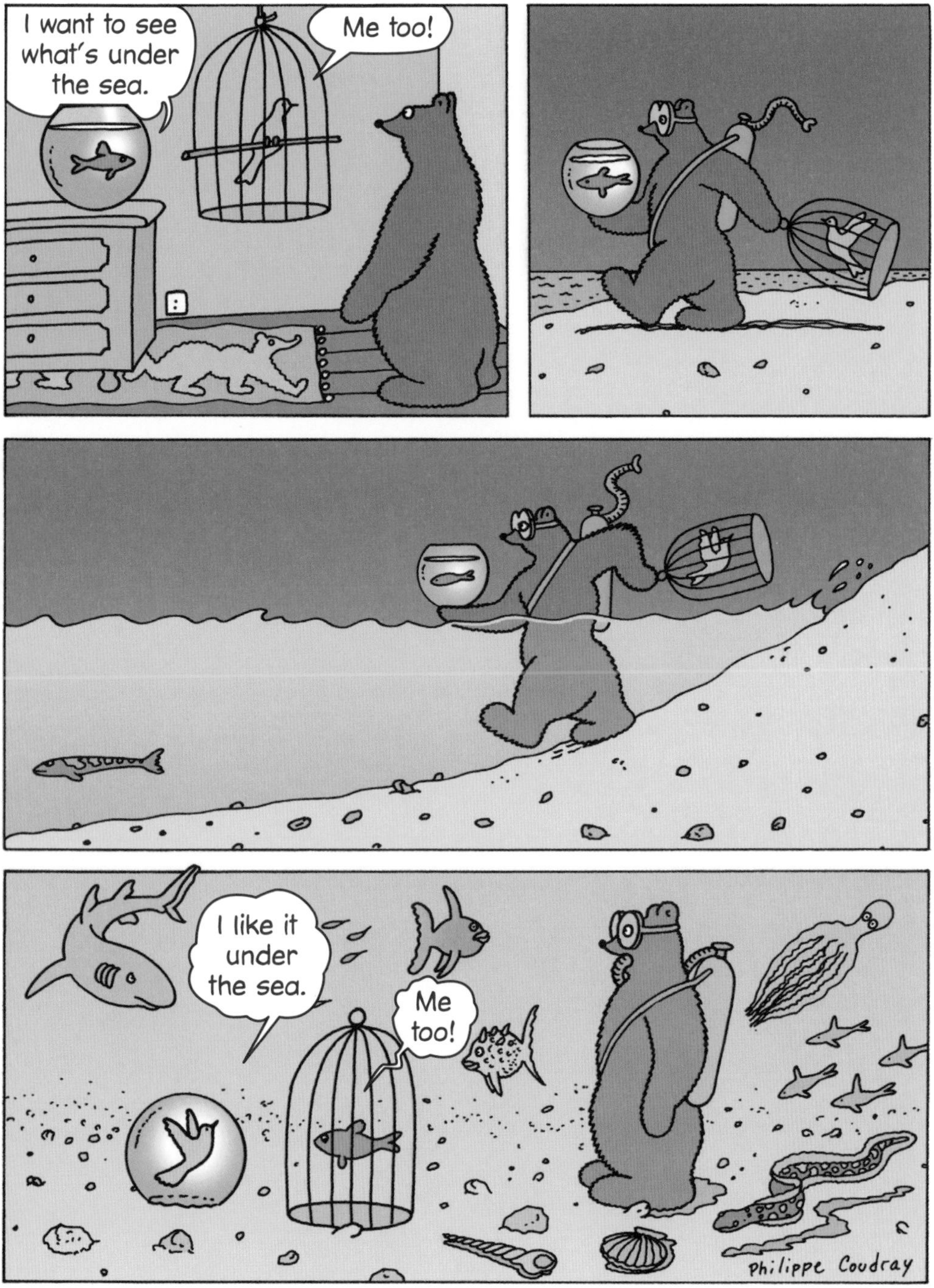
I want to see what's under the sea.
Me too!
I like it under the sea.
Me too!
Philippe Coudray

The maze

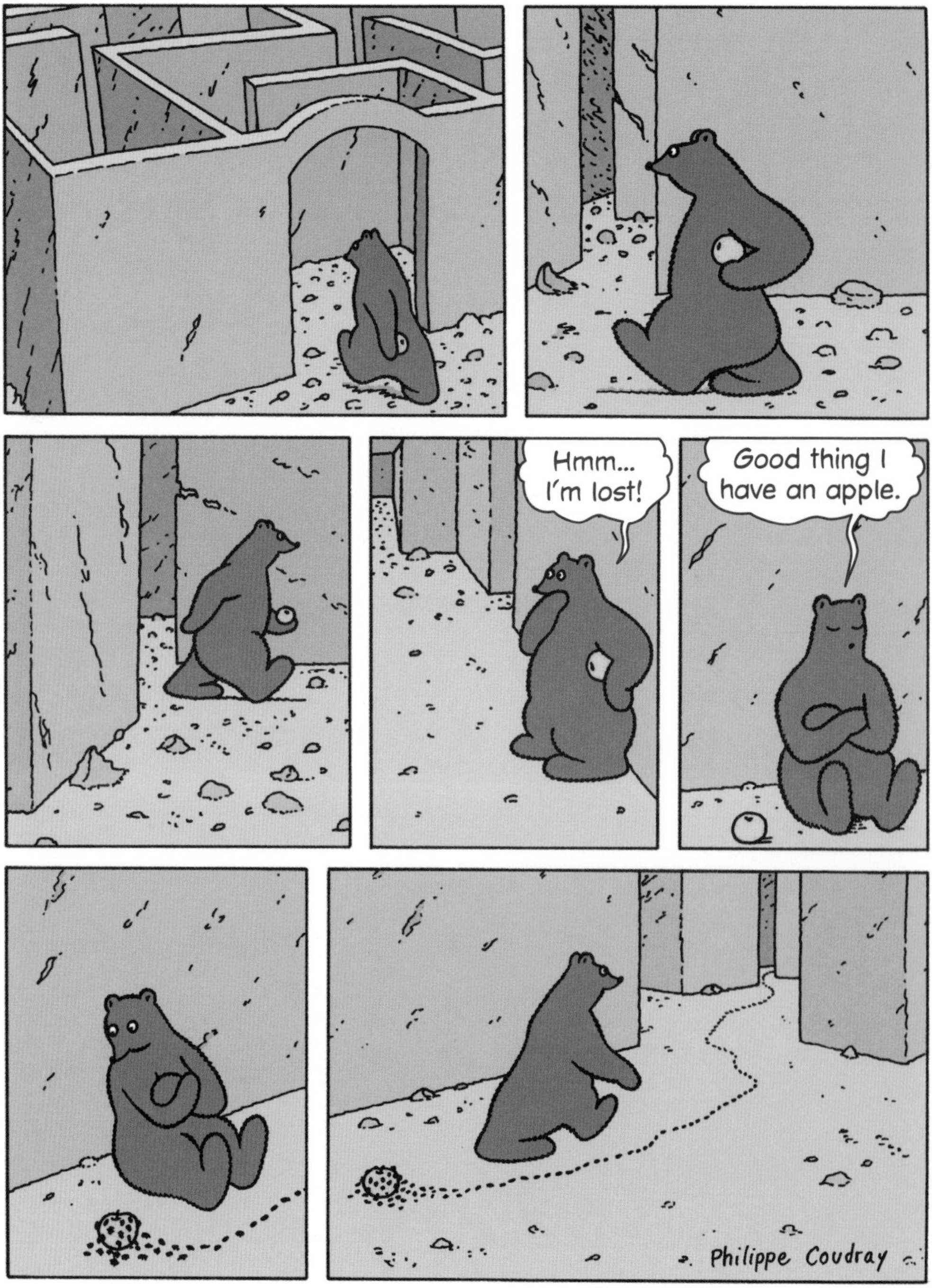
Hmm...
I'm lost!
Good thing I
have an apple.
Philippe Coudray

Help your friends

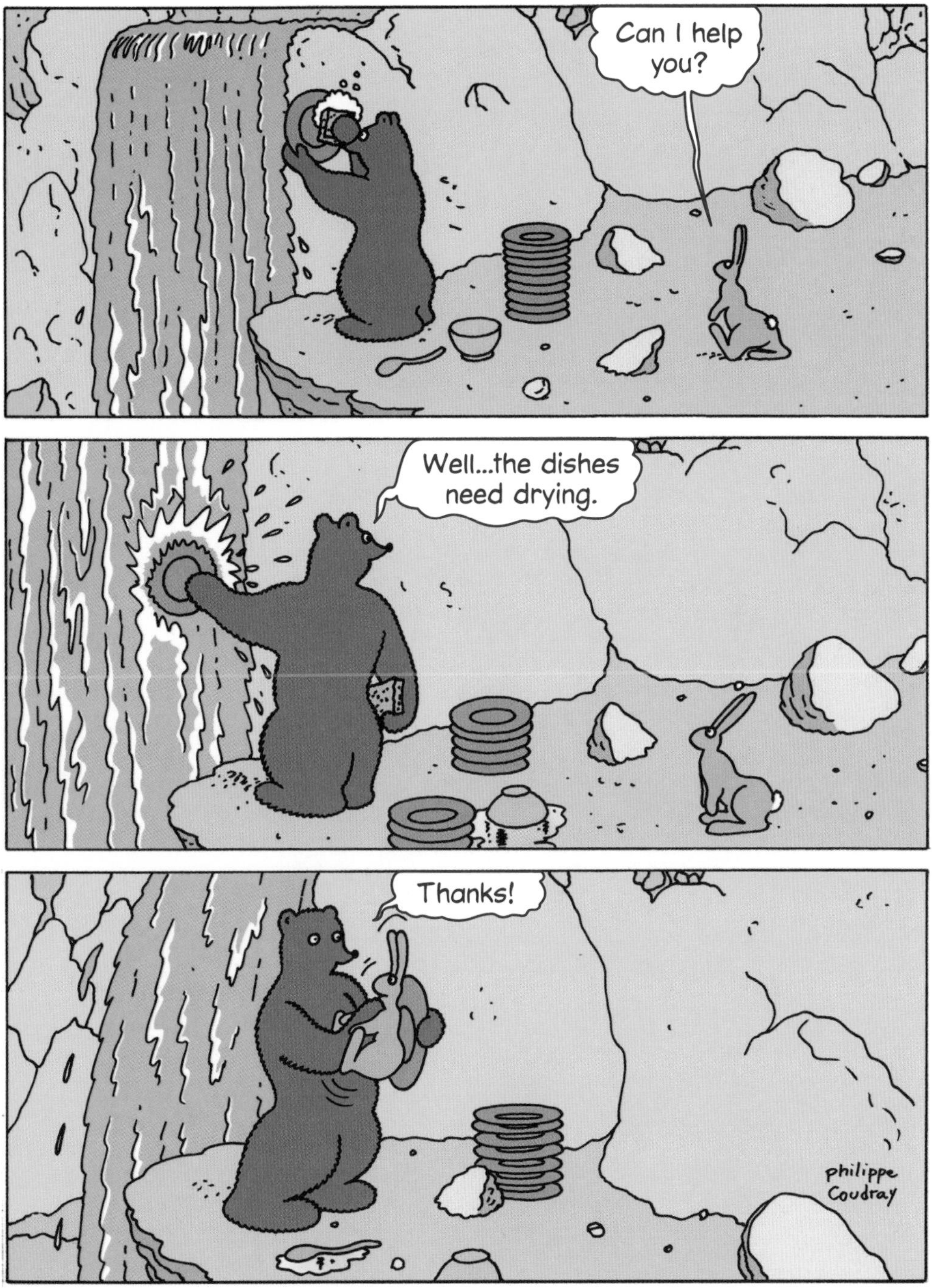
Can I help you?
Well...the dishes need drying.
Thanks!
philippe Coudray

Play with me

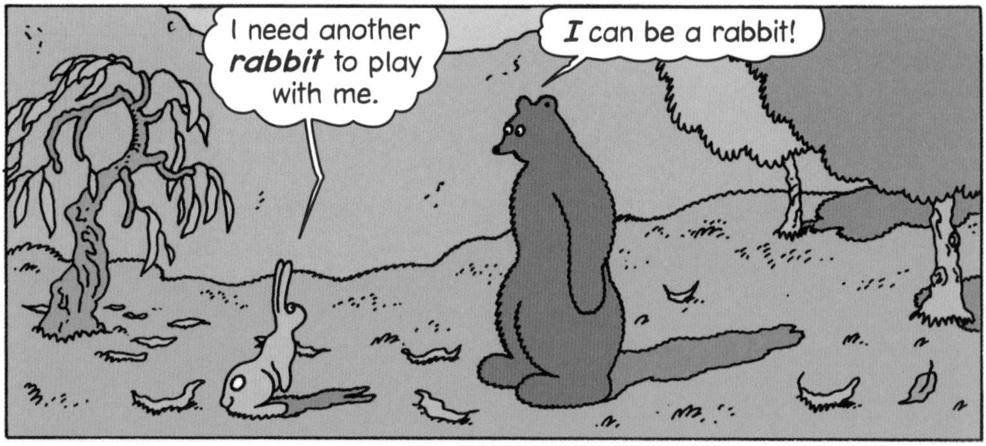
I need another *rabbit* to play with me.
I can be a rabbit!

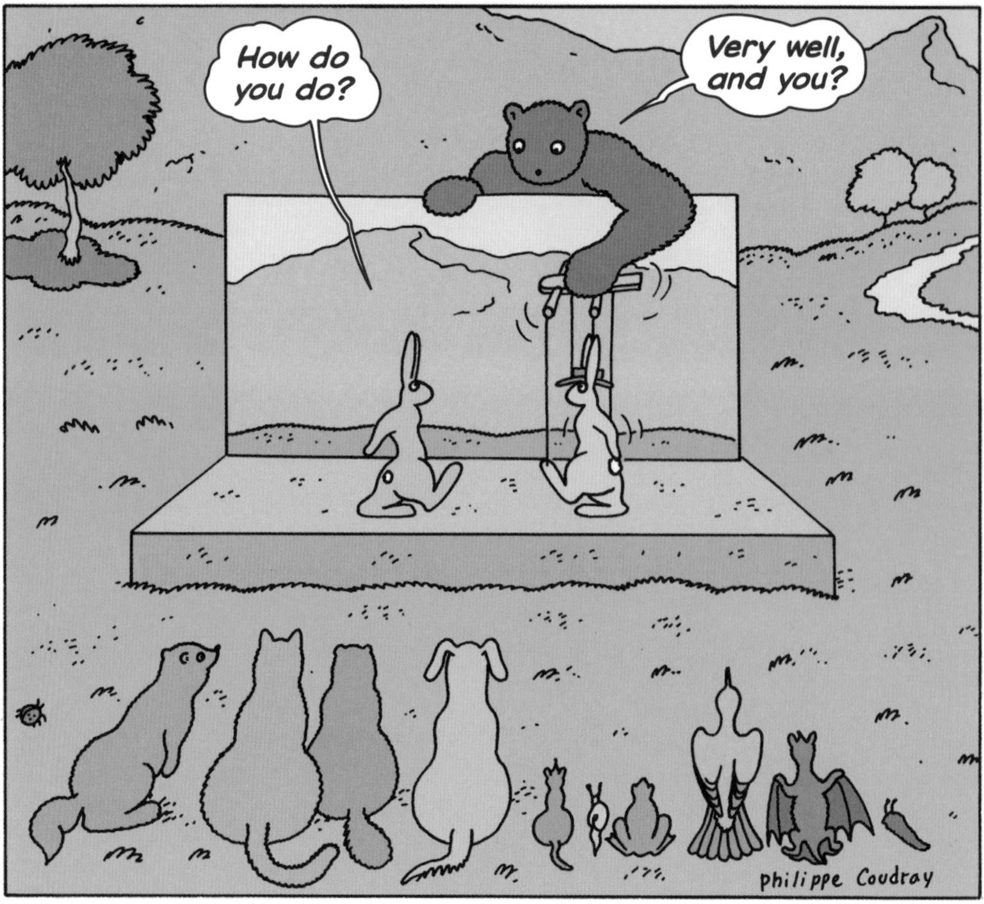
How do you do?
Very well, and you?
philippe Coudray

To jump—or not

Philippe Coudray

Sailboat

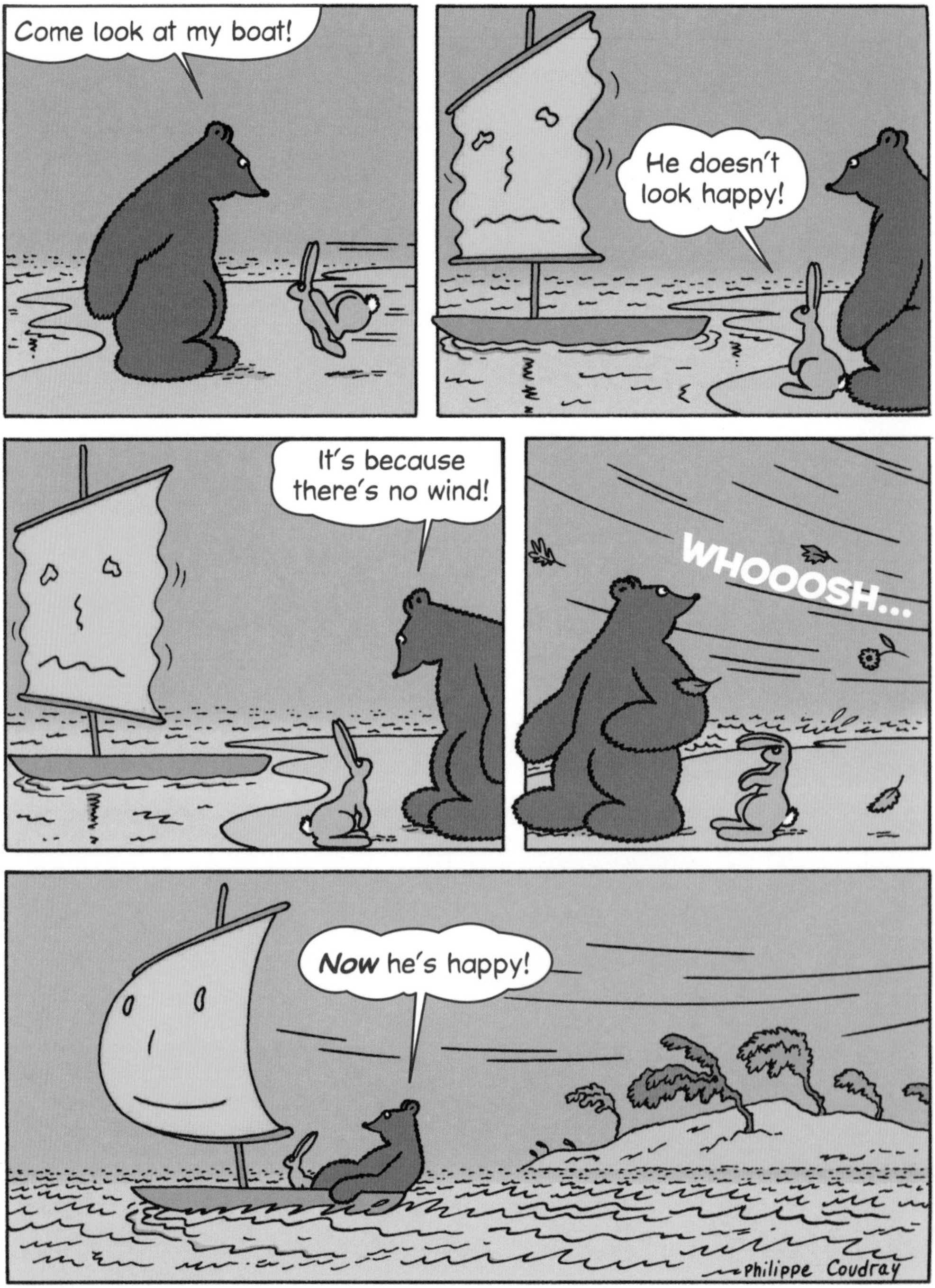
Come look at my boat!
He doesn't look happy!
It's because there's no wind!
WHOOOSH...
Now he's happy!
Philippe Coudray

At the store

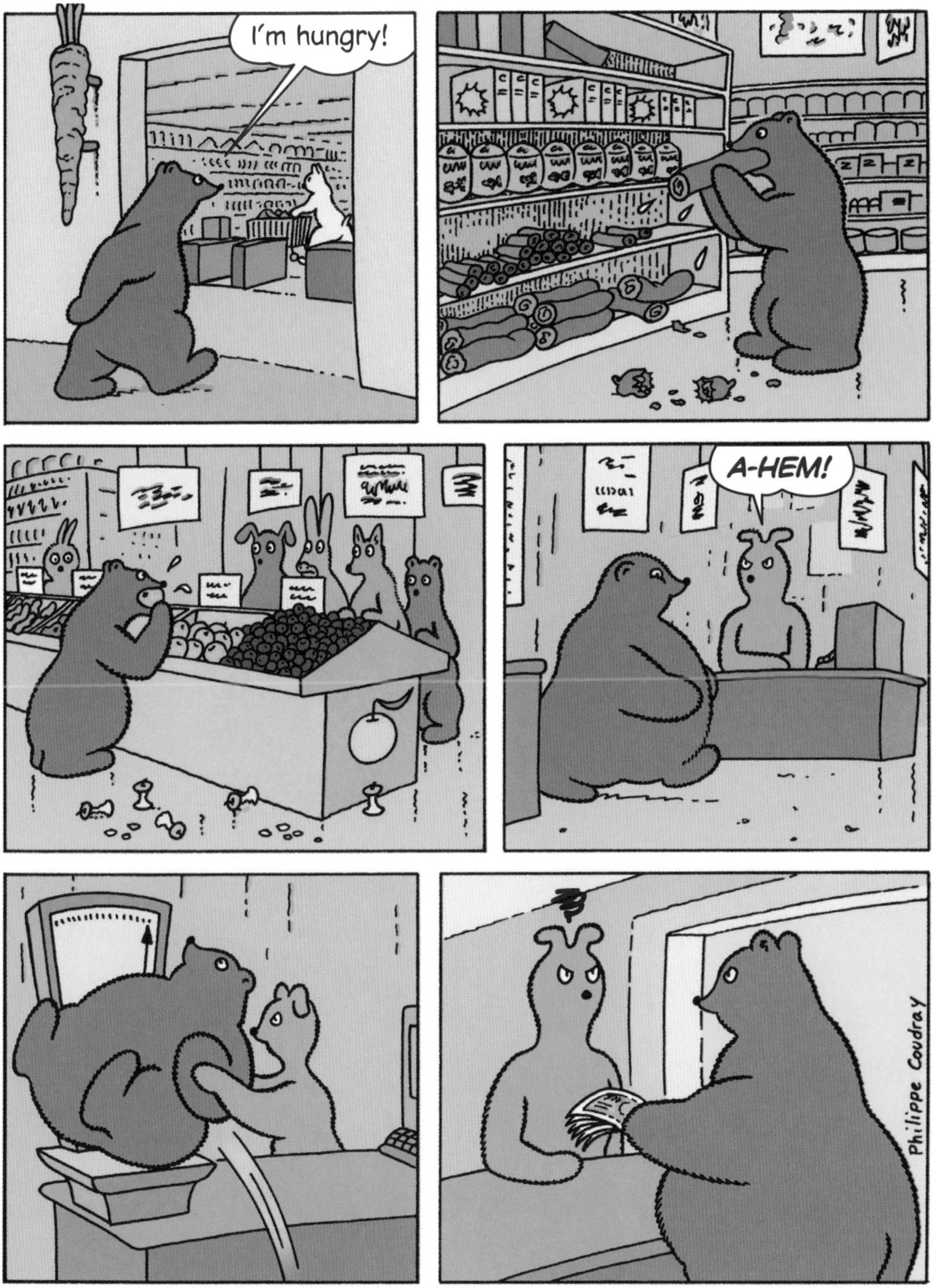
I'm hungry!
A-HEM!
Philippe Coudray

Sunset

Philippe Coudray

Winter is coming

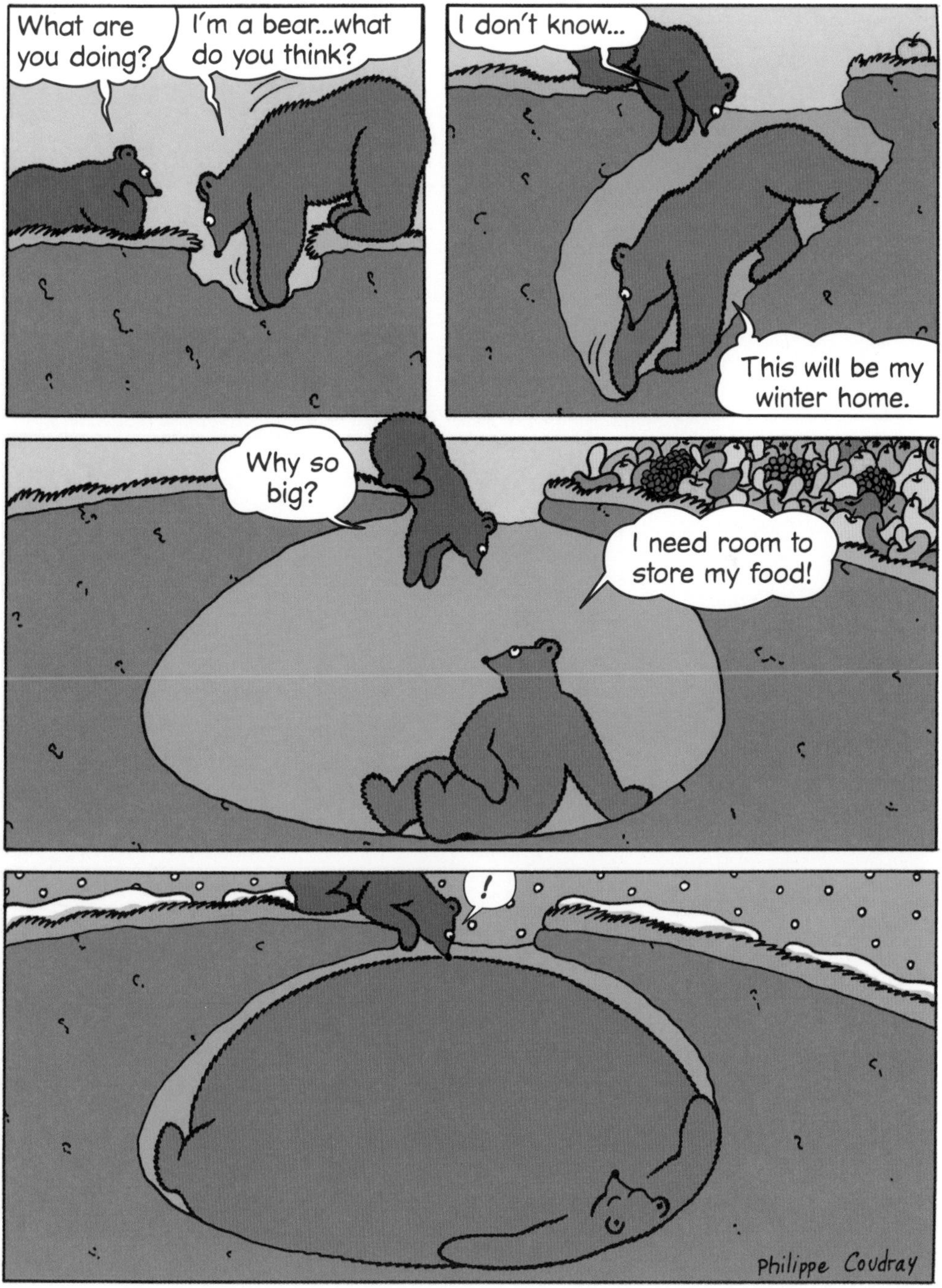

What are you doing?
I'm a bear...what do you think?
I don't know...
This will be my winter home.
Why so big?
I need room to store my food!
!
Philippe Coudray

Too much wind!

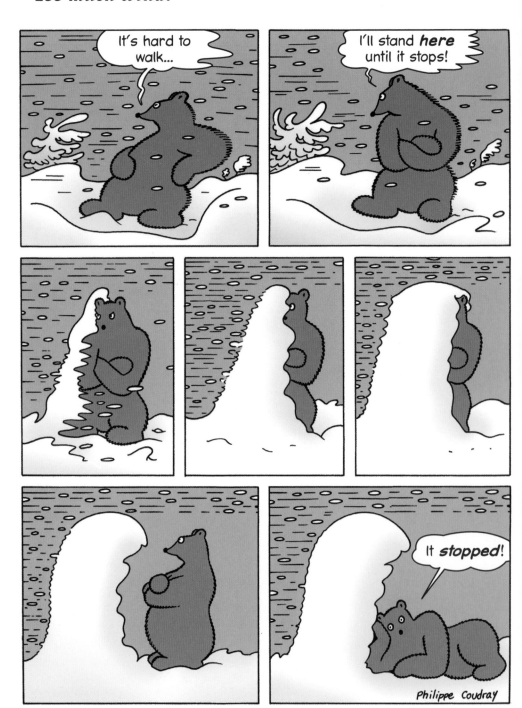

Philippe Coudray

The winner

Philippe Coudray

A good friend

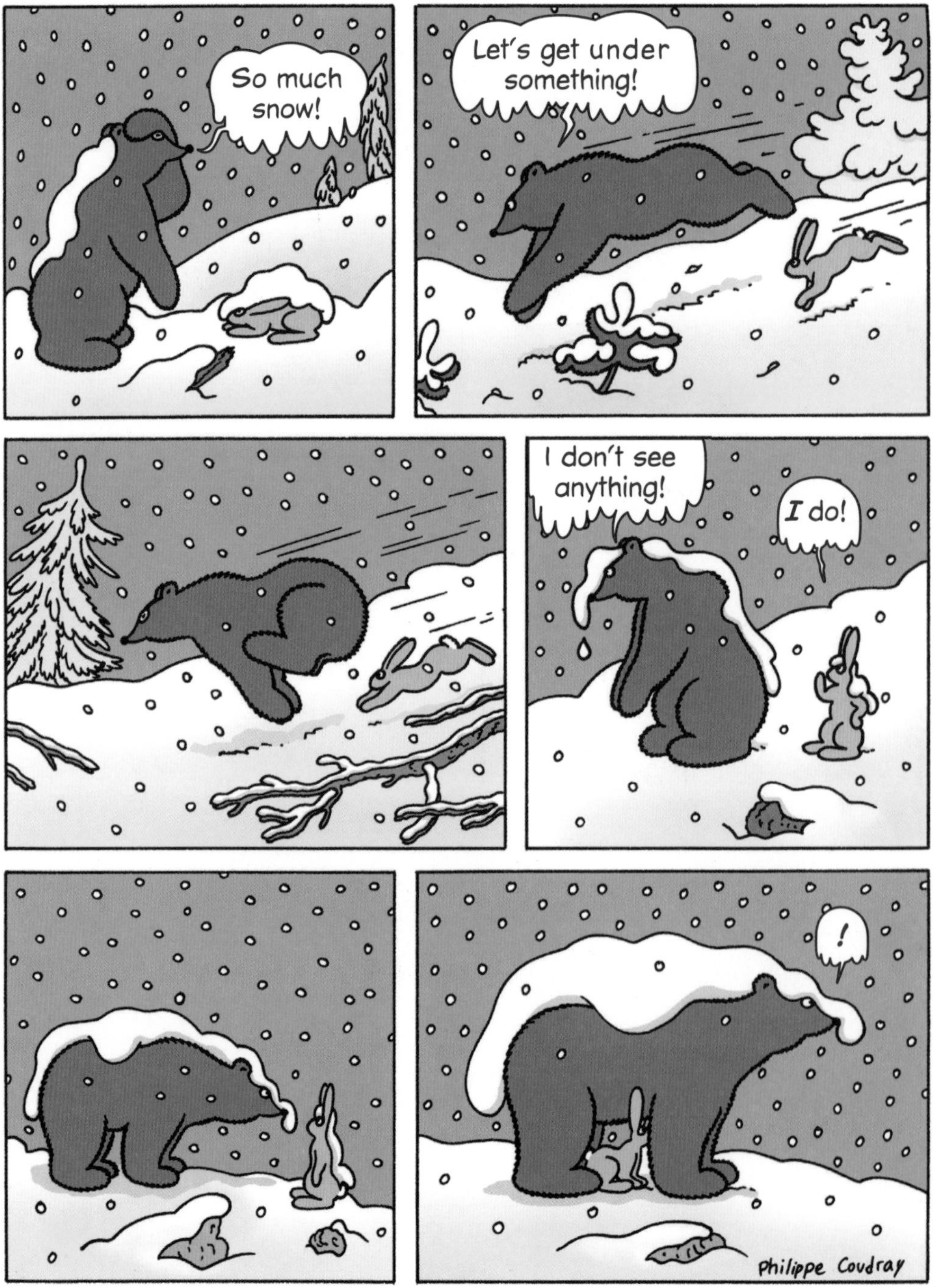

So much snow!
Let's get under something!
I don't see anything!
I do!
!
Philippe Coudray

Do as you are told!

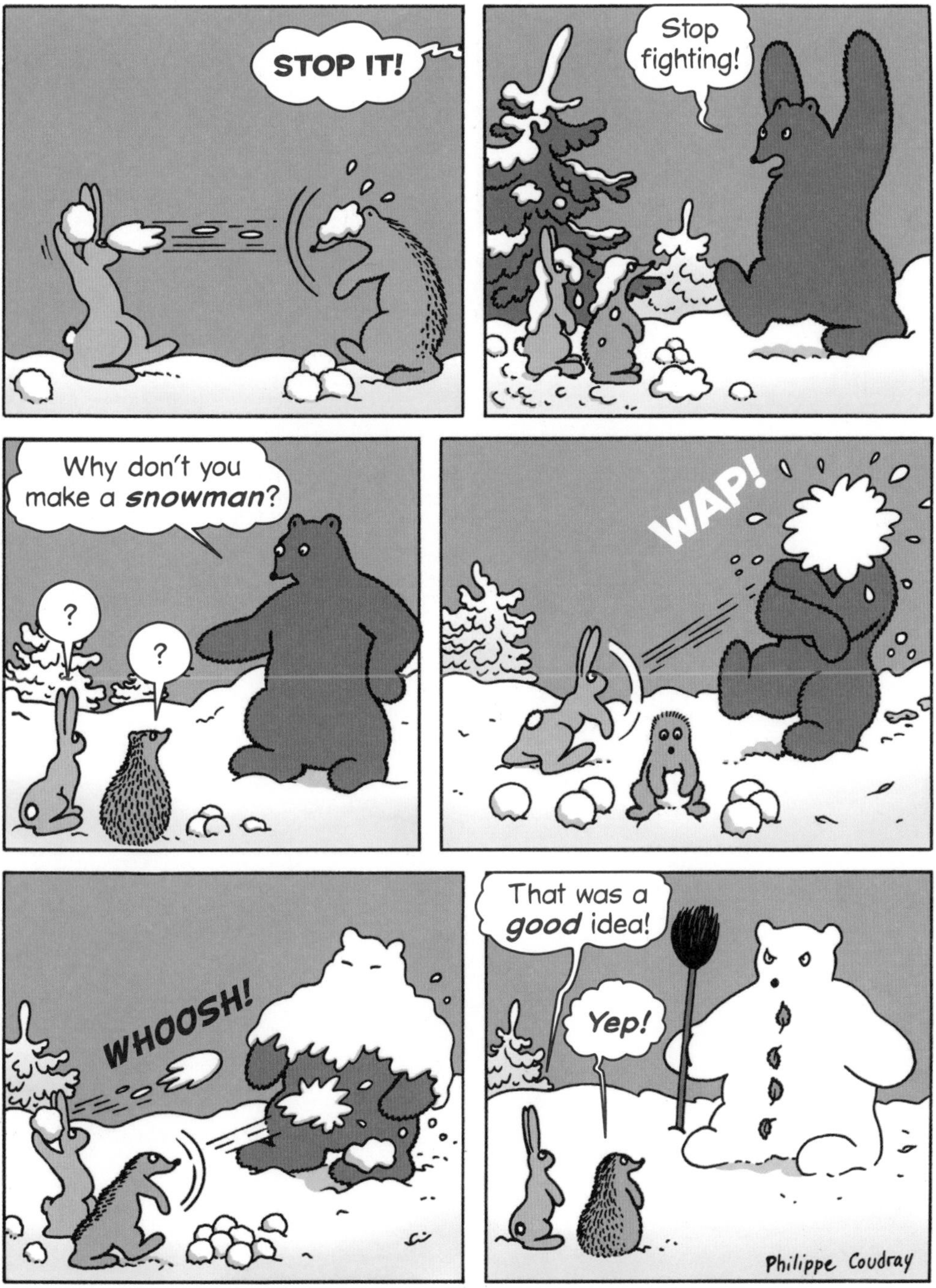
STOP IT!
Stop fighting!
Why don't you make a snowman?
?
?
WAP!
WHOOSH!
That was a good idea!
Yep!
Philippe Coudray

Friends

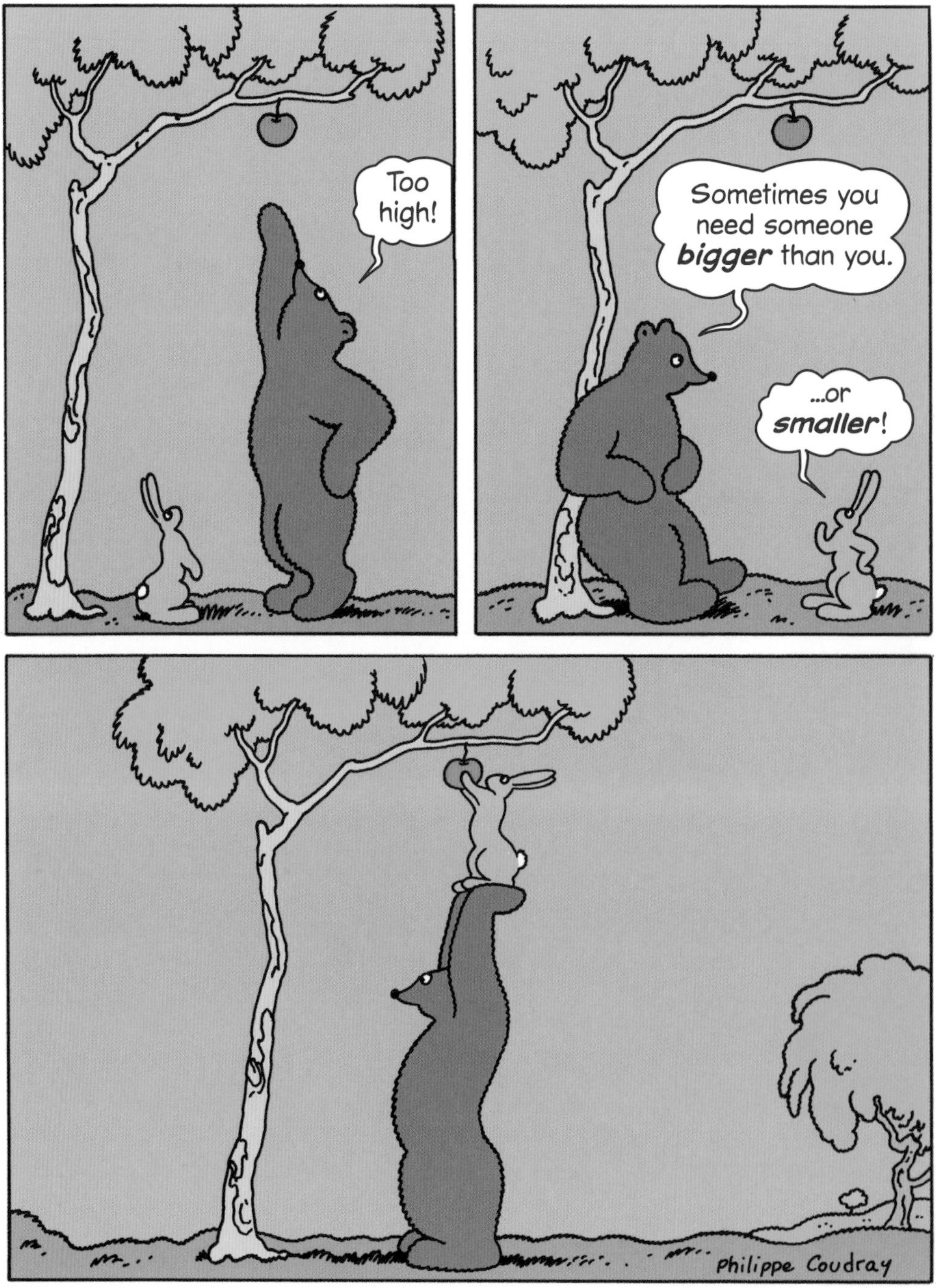
Too high!
Sometimes you need someone **bigger** than you.
...or **smaller**!
Philippe Coudray

The biggest fish

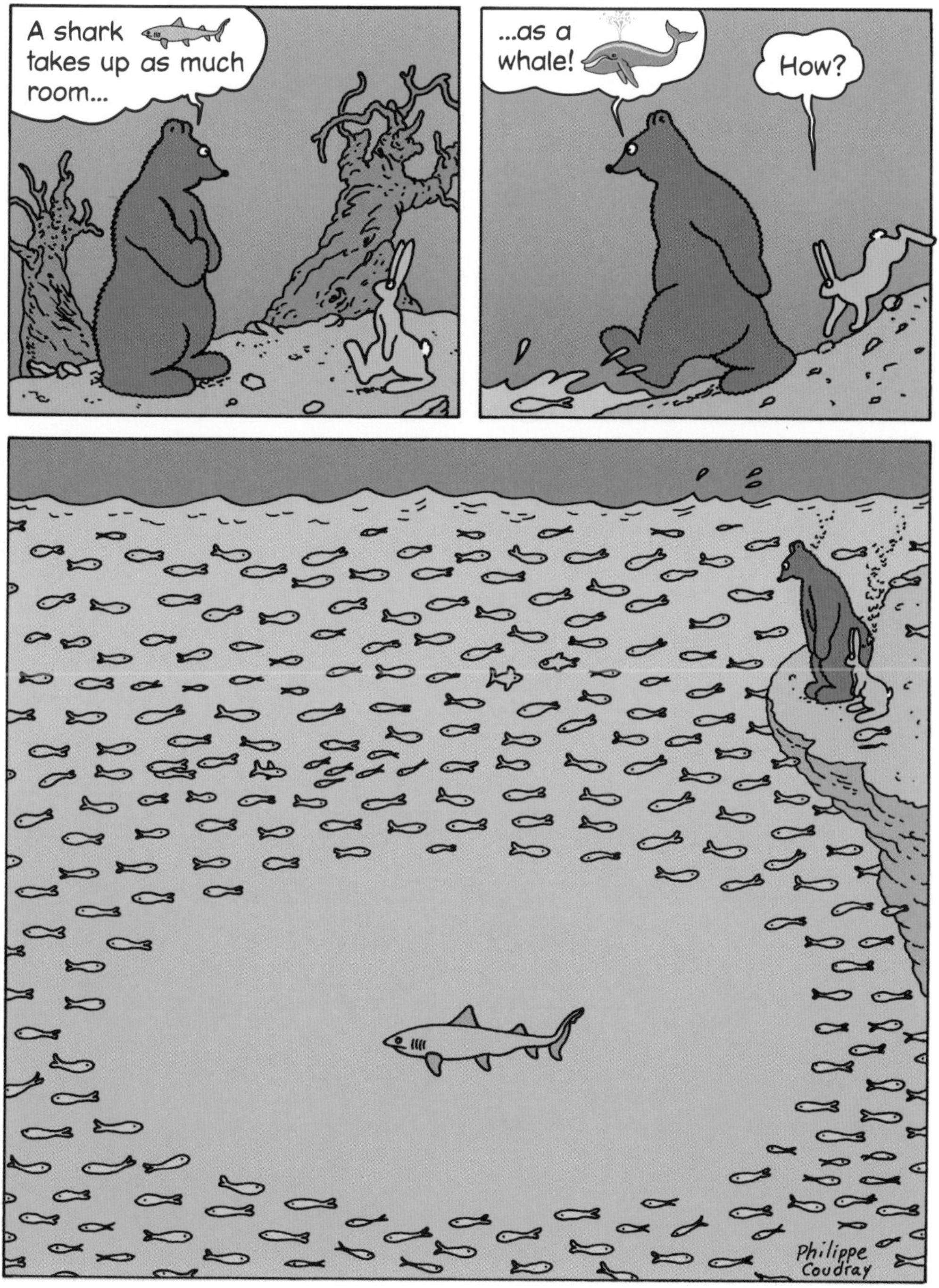
A shark takes up as much room...
...as a whale!
How?
Philippe Coudray

I want to play!

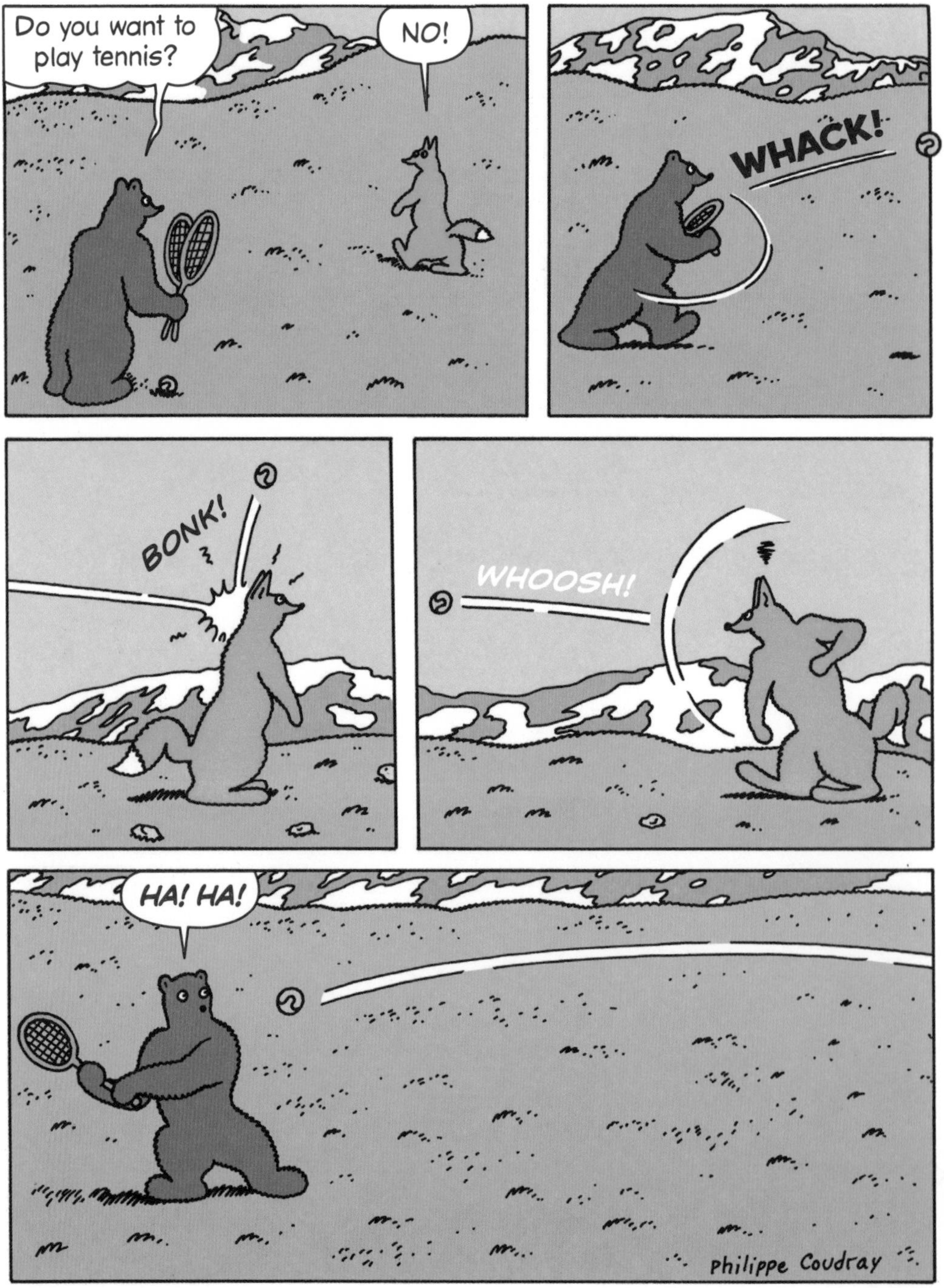
Do you want to play tennis?
NO!
WHACK!
BONK!
WHOOSH!
HA! HA!
Philippe Coudray

The hot dog

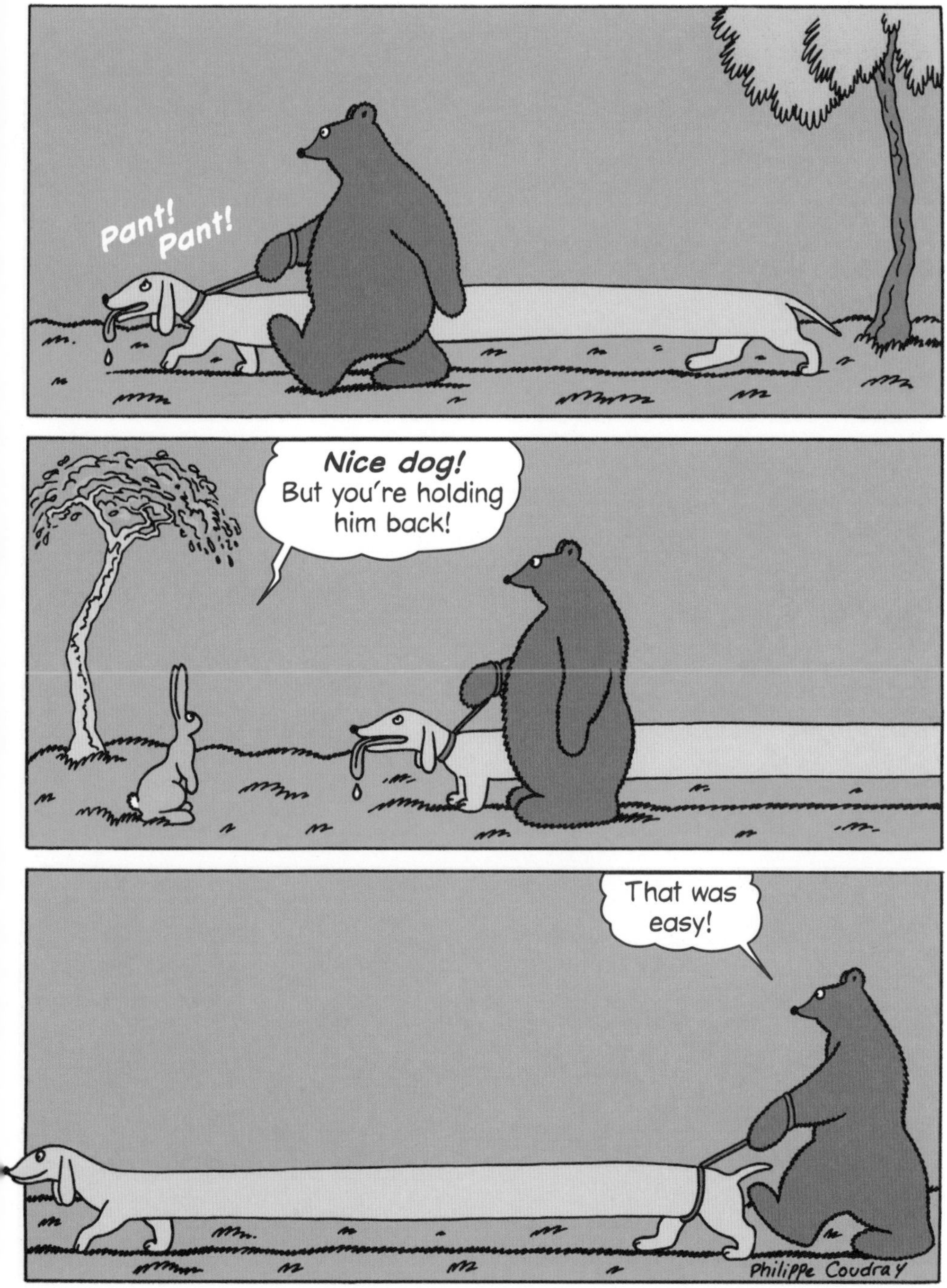
Pant!
Pant!
Nice dog!
But you're holding him back!
That was easy!
Philippe Coudray

Back to school

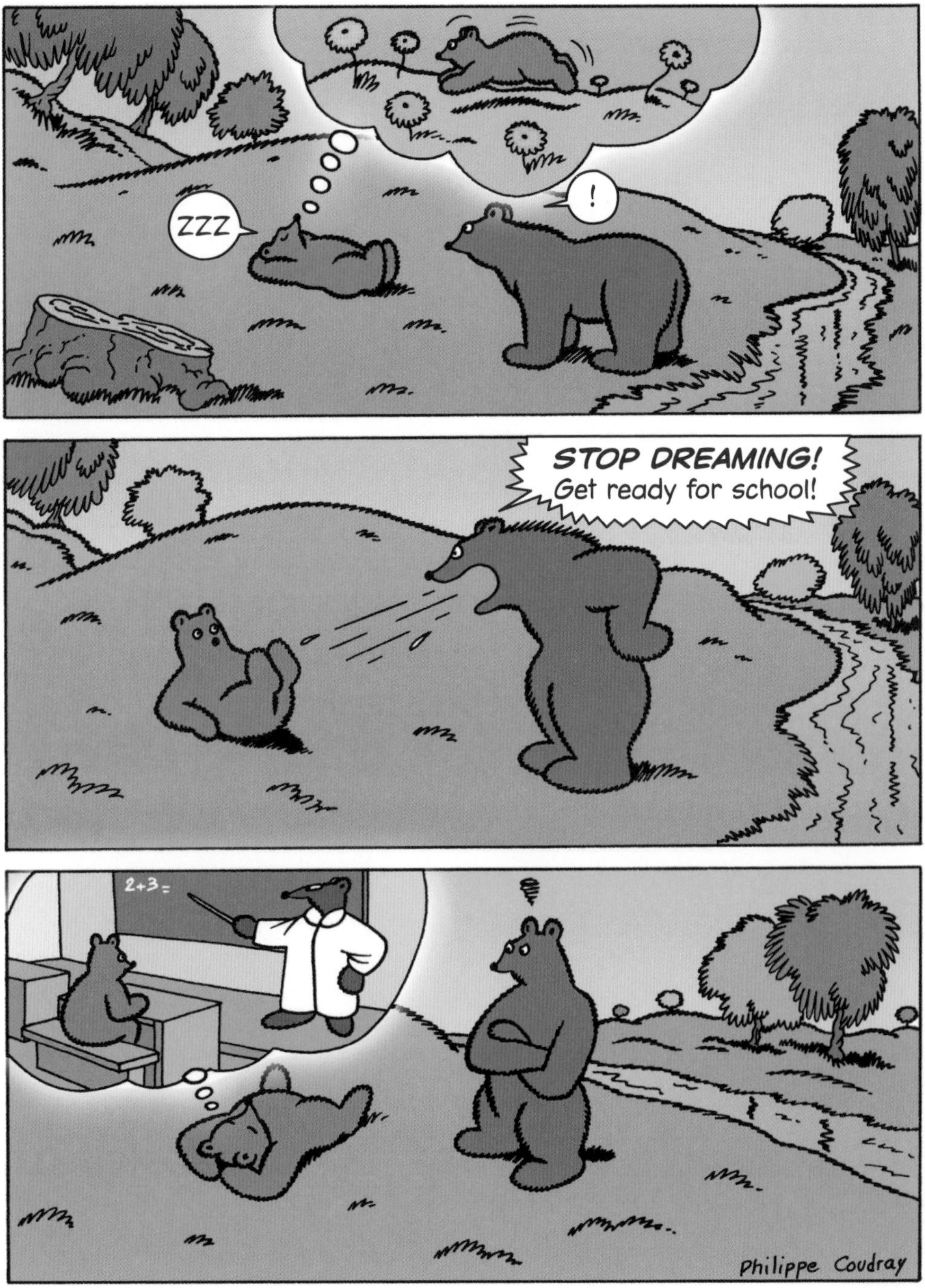
ZZZ
!
STOP DREAMING!
Get ready for school!
2+3=
Philippe Coudray

The comic strip

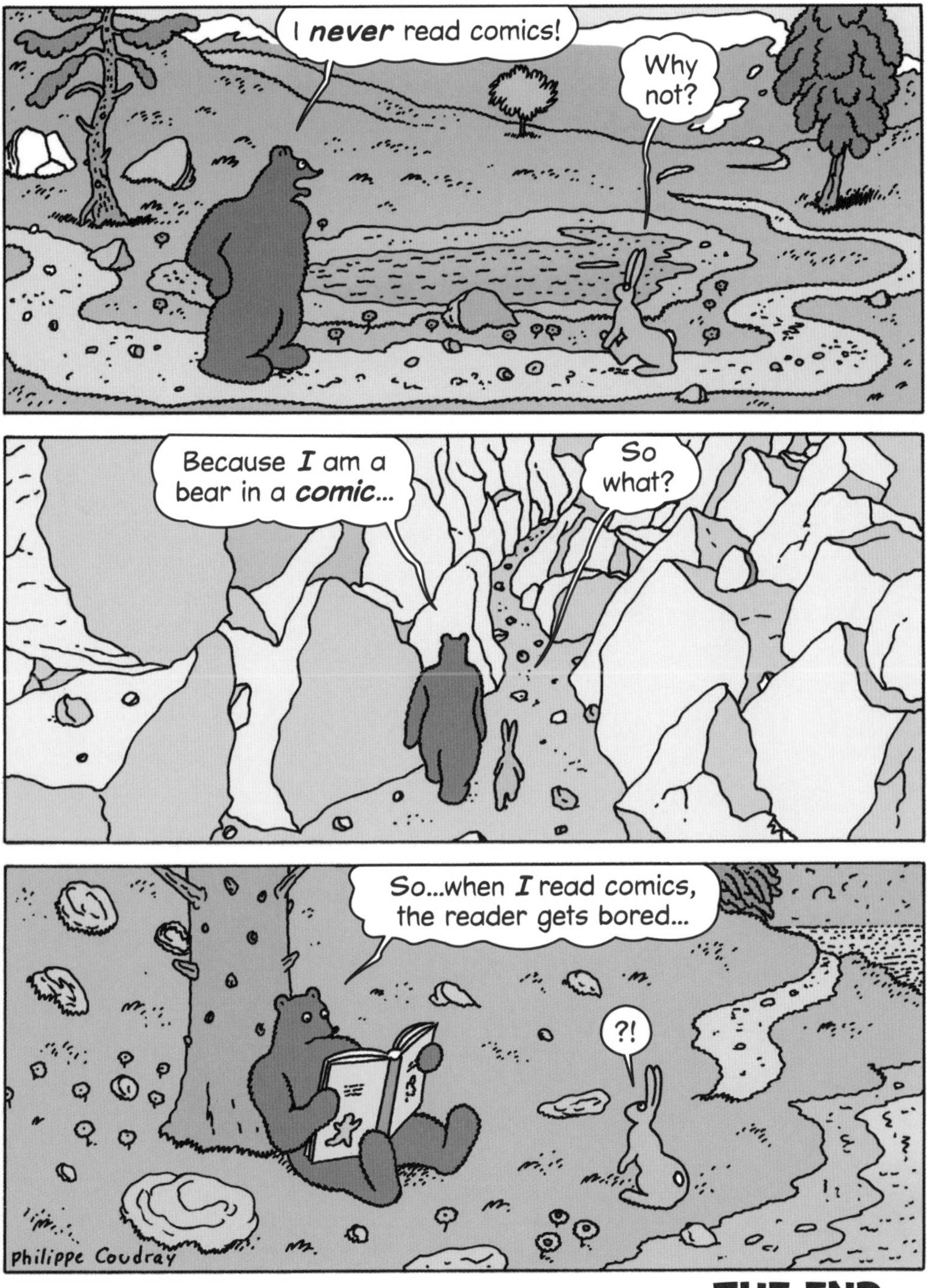
I never read comics!
Why not?
Because I am a bear in a comic...
So what?
So...when I read comics, the reader gets bored...
?!
Philippe Coudray

THE END

HOW TO "TOON INTO READING"
in a few simple steps:

Our goal is to get kids reading—and we know kids LOVE comics. We publish award-winning early readers in comics form for elementary and early middle school, and present them in three levels.

CHICK & CHICKIE
PLAY ALL DAY!
What do you want to play?
I have a great idea...
Claude Ponti
ZIG AND WIKKI
MO AND JO
FIGHTING TOGETHER FOREVER
BENNY AND PENNY
THE BIG NO-NO!
Oh, Benny, this is a very big NO-NO!
Yes!
GEOFFREY HAYES
THE SHARK KING
KIKUO JOHNSON

1 FIND THE RIGHT BOOK

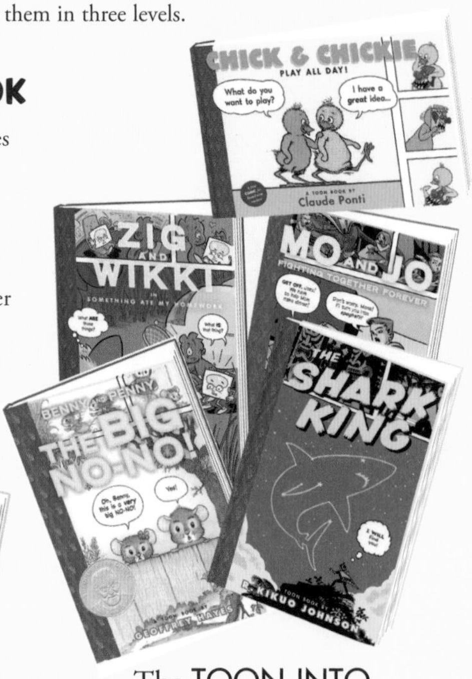

Veteran teacher Cindy Rosado tells what makes a good book for beginning and struggling readers alike: "A vetted vocabulary, plenty of picture clues, repetition, and a clear and compelling story. Also, the book shouldn't be too easy—or the reader won't learn, but neither should it be too hard—or he or she may get discouraged."

If you love Benjamin Bear, look for more of his adventures in "Bright Ideas!" and "Brain Storms!"

BENJAMIN BEAR in Bright Ideas!
PHILIPPE COUDRAY
BENJAMIN BEAR in Fuzzy Thinking
BENJAMIN BEAR in Brain Storms!
A TOON BOOK BY PHILIPPE COUDRAY

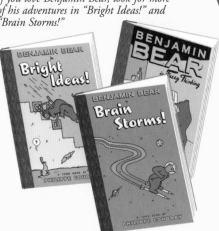

The TOON INTO READING!™ program is designed for beginning readers and works wonders with reluctant readers.

2 TAKE TIME WITH SILENT PANELS

Comics use panels to mark time, and silent panels count. Look and "read" even when there are no words. Often, humor is all in the timing!

KNOCK! KNOCK!
TRICK OR TREAT!

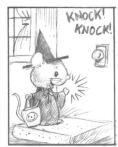

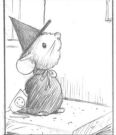

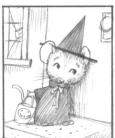

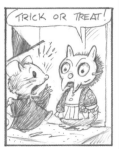

③ GUIDE YOUNG READERS

What works?
Keep your fingertip <u>below</u> the character that is speaking.

④ LET THE PICTURES TELL THE STORY

In a comic, you can often read the story even if you don't know all the words. Encourage young readers to tell you what's happening based on the facial expressions and body language.

⑤ GET OUT THE CRAYONS

Kids see the hand of the author in a comic and it makes them want to tell their own stories. Encourage them to talk, write and draw!

Get kids talking, and you'll be surprised at how perceptive they are about pictures.

⑥ LET THEM GUESS

Comics provide a large amount of context for the words, so let young readers make informed guesses, and don't over-correct. In this panel, the artist shows a pirate ship, two pirate hats, and two pirate flags the first time the word "PIRATE" is introduced.

7 HAM IT UP!

Think of the comic book story as a play, and read with expression and intonation. Assign parts or get kids to read the sound effects–a great way to reinforce phonics skills.

What works?

Even very young readers will enjoy making the easy-to-read sound effects.

8 HAVE FUN WITH BALLOONS Comics use various kinds of balloons.

SPEECH BALLOONS

THOUGHT BALLOONS

SOUND EFFECTS

9 LET THEM RE-READ Children love to read comics and to RE-read them, finding all the details that make comics so pleasurable. When they re-read, emerging and struggling readers become <u>fluent</u> readers.

10 ABOVE ALL, ENJOY!

There is, of course, never one right way to read, so go for the shared pleasure. Children who make the story happen in their imaginations have discovered the thrill of reading. At that point, just go get them more books, and more comics.

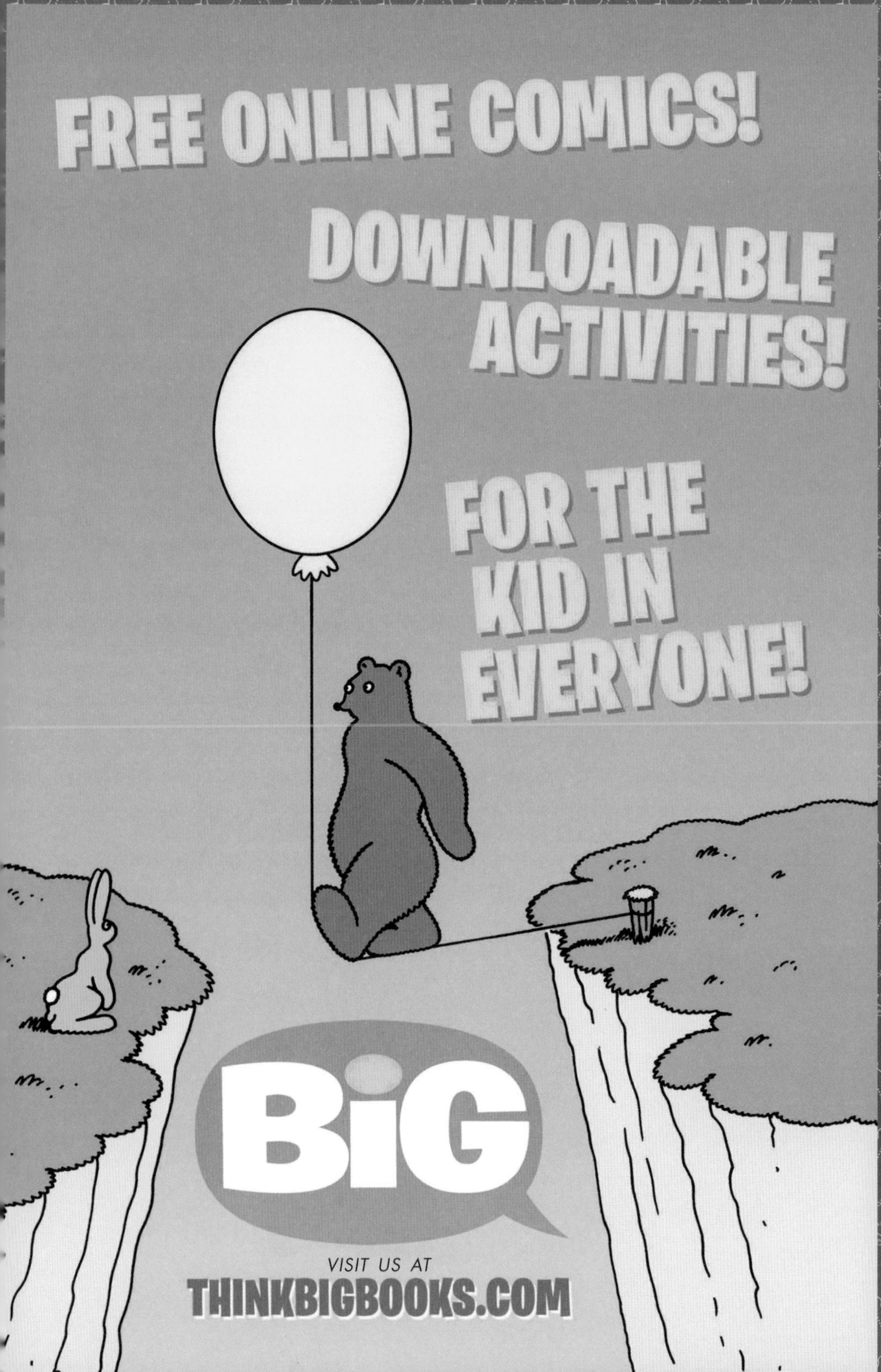
FREE ONLINE COMICS!
DOWNLOADABLE ACTIVITIES!
FOR THE KID IN EVERYONE!
BiG
VISIT US AT
THINKBIGBOOKS.COM